Paddington at the Zoo

Michael Bond

illustrated by David McKee

Collins

One day Jonathan and Judy decided to take
Paddington on an outing to the zoo.
Paddington made a large pile of marmalade
sandwiches — six in all — and they set out.

But when they came to the zoo gates, the man wouldn't let them in.

"I'm sorry," he said. "Pets aren't allowed in the zoo."

"Pets!" repeated Jonathan.

"Paddington isn't a *pet*," said Judy. "He's one of the family."

Paddington gave the man such a hard stare he let them in without further ado.

"Come on," said Jonathan, when they were inside. "Let's go and see the animals and I'll take your photograph."

"Give a great big smile," called Judy. "Say cheese!"

"Cheese," said Paddington.

"Squawk!" said the parrot, and it took a big bite out of Paddington's sandwich. "Thank you very much. Squawk! Squawk!"

Next they went to see the Siberian Wild Dog.

But the Siberian Wild Dog went "Owwowwwowwwoo!", so Paddington threw him the rest of the sandwich to keep him quiet.

"Hee! Haw!" brayed the donkey. And it wouldn't move until Paddington had given it his second marmalade sandwich.

"That's two gone," said Judy.

Paddington's smile was getting less cheesy all the time.

The elephant didn't wait to be asked. It made a loud trumpeting noise – "Whoooohoowooo!" – and then it helped itself to Paddington's third marmalade sandwich.

Paddington began to feel that going to the zoo was not such a good idea after all.

But there was worse to follow.

When the lion saw them coming, it gave a roar – "Grrrrrrrrahh!" Paddington nearly jumped out of his duffle coat with alarm.

"I think I had better give the lion a sandwich too," he said. "He sounds hungry."

"And very fierce," added Judy.

The only ones who didn't say anything were the penguins. They just stood there looking rather sad, as if they were all dressed up for a party but had nowhere to go. Paddington felt so sorry for them he gave them sandwich number five.

"Penguins eat fish," said a man sternly. He pointed to a notice. "It is strictly forbidden to give them marmalade sandwiches."

And while Paddington was looking at the notice, the man helped himself to the last sandwich. Now Paddington's sandwiches had all gone!

"The cheek of it!" said a lady. "Here . . . have some of my bread."

"Thank you very much," said Paddington. And before anyone could stop him he ate it all up.

"I don't think that's quite what the lady meant," said Judy.

"Zoos make you hungry," said Paddington firmly. "Especially this one."

Just to round things off, the mountain goat
ate Paddington's sandwich bag!

"That does it!" said Jonathan. "I think
we'd better go home before anything else
happens."

A few days later Jonathan showed Paddington the photographs he'd taken at the zoo. "You can have one for your scrap book," he said.

"Which do you like best?" asked Judy.

"The one with the parrot," said Paddington promptly.

"At least the parrot said 'thank you' when he ate my marmalade sandwich. That's more than any of the others did."